Bug in a Rug

Jamie Gilson

Illustrated by Diane de Groat

Clarion Books

NEW YORK

Clarion Books
a Houghton Mifflin Company imprint
215 Park Avenue South, New York, NY 10003
Text copyright © 1998 by Jamie Gilson
Illustrations copyright © 1998 by Diane de Groat

The text is set in 14/19 pt. Palatino.
The illustrations are executed in pencil on paper.

Printed in the U.S.A.

Library of Congress Cataloging-in-Publication Data

Gilson, Jamie.
Bug in a rug / Jamie Gilson.
p.   cm.
Summary: Seven-year-old Richard is self-conscious when he
receives a pair of purple pants from his aunt and uncle and has to
wear them to school, but he is even more worried when his
uncle shows up for a visit to his classroom.
ISBN 0-395-86616-2
[1. School—Fiction.   2. Clothing and dress—Fiction.   3. Uncles—Fiction.]
I. Title.
PZ7.G4385Bu   1998
[Fic]—dc21
97-16437
CIP   AC

BP 10 9 8 7 6 5 4 3 2 1

To Holly and Matthew, bugs in a rug

Contents

1. Who's There? • 1

2. Way, Way, Way! • 12

3. Squirms • 23

4. Larva Legs • 32

5. I Didn't Mean To • 42

6. Uncle Ken, Meet Uncle Ken • 49

7. A Holdup • 58

1.

Who's There?

"Little Richie, you are as cute as a bug in a rug." Aunt Nannie squeezed me.

"My name is Richard," I told her. And I was almost as big as she was.

She laughed and squeezed me again, harder. If I was toothpaste, my cap would have popped.

"Hey, big fella." Uncle Ken messed up my hair. He and Aunt Nannie were driving their red van all the way from Texas to Alaska. On the way, they were staying at people's houses. Our house was one of them.

"Cousin Mae just begged us to stay another week," Aunt Nannie said, "but Ken said no, it was time he saw little Richie. And you, too, my dear." She hugged my mom.

"We left there at dawn's early light," Uncle Ken said.

He set their fat suitcase on the hall rug. With his cowboy hat on, he was almost as tall as the front door. "Knock, knock," he said to me.

"I've got to go to school now," I told him.

He shook his head. "When I say, 'Knock, knock,' you've got to say, 'Who's there?'"

I knew that. I know knock-knock jokes.

"Knock, knock," he said again.

When big people meet you they mostly say, "My, how you've grown." They don't say, "Knock, knock."

"Okay. Who's there?" I asked.

"Ken," he said.

But that's who he *was*. He was my Uncle Ken.

"When you do a knock-knock, you're not supposed to use your real name," I told him.

Mom turned and looked at me hard, like I'd said the wrong thing.

So I kept it going. "Okay. Ken who?" I asked him.

"*Ken*'t you guess?" he said. And he laughed, "Huf, huf, huf."

It was only a little funny. I bet he'd told it before. Uncle Ken was laughing a lot anyway. Mom laughed, too.

Aunt Nannie didn't. "My, how you've grown," she said. "And so sweet. Your little cousins in Memphis are rascals. We spent three days with them."

"Two days too many, if you ask me," Uncle Ken said.

"But the last time we saw little Richie," Aunt Nannie went on, "he wasn't even potty trained. How long has it been, Ellen?" she asked my mom. "Three years?"

Three years ago I was four. I hope by *then* I was potty trained.

"Longer," my mother said. "Richard's in second grade now. The last time you were here he was just a baby."

"Oh, and *such* a baby. He's the spitting image of Ken's baby pictures," Aunt Nannie said. "Look at those eyes."

I looked at Uncle Ken. He had one head. I had one head. He had two eyes. I had two eyes. That was about it. I wondered what a spitting image *was,* anyway.

Uncle Ken is my dad's brother. People say I'm the spitting image of my dad, too. He lives in Seattle. I get to see him every summer and at Christmas. Seattle is a long way from Illinois, so that's why I don't see him more.

"*So* cute." Aunt Nannie headed for me, her arms out for another hug.

I ducked. In one second flat I got to the front door. I grabbed my schoolbook about bats. "Bye," I said.

"No, you don't, Richard," Mom told me. "It's time for breakfast, not the bus. Come along, Nannie," she went on. "I'll get you settled before Richard and I have to go. I've made a list of places you might visit until we're back—the mall, the nature museum, Green Lake."

She picked up their suitcase. "Your room's upstairs."

It wasn't their room. It was mine. Aunt Nannie and Uncle Ken were going to sleep in my new bunk bed. What I'd get is my blue blanket on the living-room sofa.

"I'm not hungry," I said, and I opened the front door.

"In an hour you will be," Mom called back, and she started up the steps with Aunt Nannie. "It's on the table."

Uncle Ken followed me into the kitchen. "What's for breakfast?" he asked.

Breakfast was a banana and Berry B'oats. Berry B'oats are my new favorite cereal. They're oats, but they taste like berries and they look like little pink tugboats floating in your milk.

"You want some?" I asked him. "I'll get another bowl."

"No," he said. "We ate eggs at Cousin Mae's.

I'll just watch." And he did. He sat down and he watched.

First he watched me peel the banana.

It was a big banana. I stuffed half of it into my mouth so I wouldn't have to talk.

"So, what do you call that stuff between your teeth?" he asked me.

I puffed out my cheeks, chewed slow, and shook my head.

"You ever eat a banana split?" he asked. "Well, that's a banana *splat!*" He slapped his knee and laughed, "Huf, huf, huf."

I would have laughed, too, just to be nice, but I'd have sprayed him with chewed banana, and that would have been a banana *spit.*

I poured my bowl half full of milk. Then I sprinkled in a whole fleet of Berry B'oats. I scooped up a mouthful, crunched them into little pieces, and swallowed them down. Then I cut in some banana slices and stirred them around. The pink oatmeal boats crashed on my banana islands.

Uncle Ken grinned. "You know what's best in Berry B'oats?" he asked.

I took a huge banana–Berry B'oat bite.

"Your teeth," he said. "*That's* what's best in Berry B'oats, your teeth." And he huffed some more.

"You've got a funny little guy here," he said to my mom when she and Aunt Nannie came into the kitchen. "He's a laugh a minute."

"He's the image of you," Aunt Nannie said. She was holding a present. It was wrapped in blue and yellow bunny paper.

"For our little Richie," she said. "I made it myself."

That probably meant it wasn't a skateboard.

I tore the bunny paper off anyway. I was right. It wasn't anywhere near a skateboard.

I held it up. It looked like a clown suit.

"Oh," Mom said, "purple corduroy pants. Wow! That's really fun, isn't it, Richard?"

"I wasn't sure about the size," Aunt Nannie told me. "Try them on."

They were the most purple pants I'd ever seen. I hated them. I didn't want to try them on.

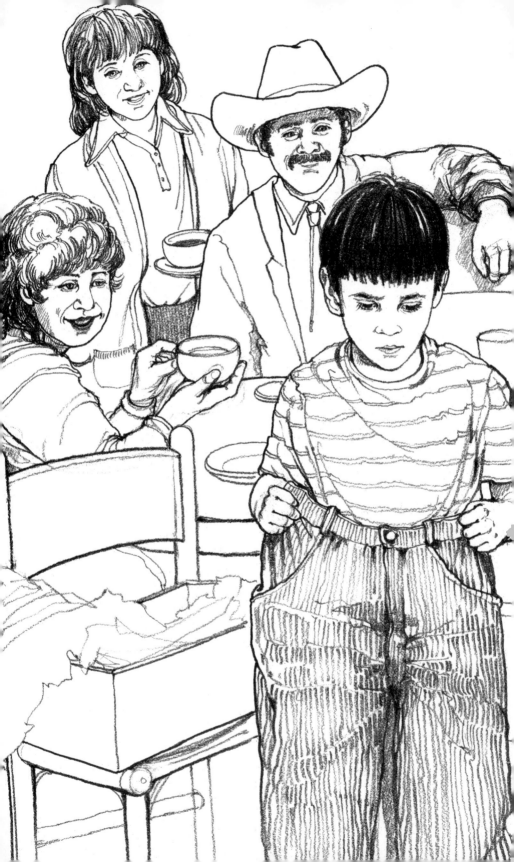

"You know how to tell a purple elephant from a . . ."

Uncle Ken was telling another joke. I ran into the bathroom with the pants.

"And wash your face," Mom said. "You have cereal on your nose and banana on your chin."

I rubbed the stuff off my face and turned the water on in the sink so it would sound like I was washing. Then I sat down on the toilet lid to think.

"Come out so I can see," Aunt Nannie called. "I made them extra big so you can grow into them."

"Hurry, honey," Mom said. "It's getting late."

There was no way out. I pulled off my jeans and pulled on the purples. They were too long, so I rolled up the legs. Then I opened the bathroom door just a crack.

"Richard," Mom said, "you've only got five minutes to make your bus."

Aunt Nannie opened the door wider. "Look at him. Turn around, sweetie. Is he not Ken all over again! They aren't too bright, are they? I know little boys like bright colors."

I turned around and then slammed the bathroom door. The water was still running hard. It was splashing over the edge of the sink. I turned it off.

Then I looked in the long mirror on the door. I looked like a humongous grape.

"I'm putting my jeans back on," I called.

But when I grabbed them off the floor they felt heavy. That's because they'd been sitting in a waterfall. My jeans were dripping all over me. I dropped them into the tub. I had to get dry ones.

"No, no, no, Richard, it's just *three* minutes," Mom called. "You don't have time to change."

I'd got the purple pants a little wet. But the jeans were soaked. I could get dry jeans, but I'd miss the bus. If I missed the bus, I'd have to walk. Then I'd be late for school. I could be late. I *could*. But I was Teacher's Pet for the day, and Mrs. Zookey had something special for me to do.

If I missed the bus, Mom could say, "Oh, that's all right. You just stay home and keep your Aunt Nannie and Uncle Ken company. Just this once." She could say that.

I left the purple pants on. I left the wet jeans in the tub. I ran out of the bathroom.

Mom held the front door open. She gave me my bat book.

I raced down the front steps. The bus was coming.

At the sidewalk I turned around. They were all waving goodbye.

I couldn't wave back. One hand was holding my book.

I hadn't put on a belt. So my other hand was holding up the purple pants.

They were too big.

Way too big.

Way.

2.

Way, Way, Way!

My name was on the chalkboard in Mrs. Zookey's room. That was good. I liked being Teacher's Pet. One thing Teacher's Pet gets to do is lead the Pledge of Allegiance to the flag of the United States of America. When you do that, you hold one hand over your heart. I did it.

With the other hand I held up my purple pants.

When we finished with "liberty and justice for all," the rest of the kids sat down. Some of them were looking at me funny, so I said, "Okay, I have to say something."

"Yes, Richard?" Mrs. Zookey asked.

"I didn't pick out these pants."

Kids giggled.

"What it is, is, my aunt and uncle are at my house," I told them. "They are these space aliens from Pluto. It's a purple planet and everybody there wears purple. They're the ones who gave me these pants. My mom made me wear them."

"They must be big around the middle on Pluto," one kid said, and he laughed.

"How long are your aunt and uncle with you?" Mrs. Zookey asked, like I'd said they were from Kansas City.

"Do they have long feelers and big hairy ears?" Yolanda asked. She giggled, too.

"They're leaving the day after tomorrow," I told them. "In their spaceship. They're going to Alaska."

Patrick laughed. "If they're your aunt and uncle," he said, "you know what that makes you? That makes you part Pluto purple person. I can say that ten times. Part Pluto purple person. Plart Puto . . ."

"Anybody else have an announcement?" Mrs. Zookey asked.

Nobody did.

"Well," she said, "as you know, this is going to be a busy day, especially for you, Richard. Today we're starting to study mealworms and how they grow and change."

Teacher's Pet got to be in charge of mealworms.

"All right, Richard," Mrs. Zookey said, "you need to pick someone to help you."

I'd already picked. "Dawn Marie," I said.

Dawn Marie smiled. She sits with me at Table Two.

So do Patrick and Sarah. I didn't pick Sarah because she was at the dentist. And Patrick was trouble. Besides, Dawn Marie said if I chose her she'd give me two handfuls of her popcorn at snack time.

"While the rest of us are talking about the day," Mrs. Zookey said, "you and Dawn Marie put the mealworms into the petri dishes. Each person gets five."

I clutched my pants and went to the worktable in the back of the room.

There are twenty-three kids in our class. There were twenty-three clear, flat plastic dishes with rims on them. Each dish had a lid. Each lid had a kid's name taped on top.

Dawn Marie grabbed the mealworm carton. "I'll do the worms," she said. "You do the oatmeal and apple part." That was okay by me.

Mrs. Zookey had cut an apple into little chunks. I put one chunk into each petri dish. Then I sprinkled in a spoonful of oatmeal. Not as yummy as Berry B'oats, I bet.

Dawn Marie stirred inside the carton with her finger. "This isn't yucky at all," she said. But it was.

She made sure I watched as she picked out the small yellowish worms by their tails or by their heads. Then she dropped them one by one into the dishes.

"One. Two. Three. Four. Five. Mrs. Zookey," she called across the room, "they aren't all the same size."

"That's right," Mrs. Zookey called back.

"What do they feel like?" I asked Dawn Marie.

"Squirmy," she said.

"Won't they die? I mean, worms are supposed to live in the ground."

"These don't." She counted out five more. "This kind live in oatmeal. And they grow and they grow and they grow until they turn into big fat rattlesnakes."

"Really?"

"Richard, have you and Dawn Marie finished?" Mrs. Zookey asked us. "You seem to be talking more than working."

"Almost," I said. "Are these things baby rattlesnakes?"

"Do *you* think so?" she asked me.

I shook my head no.

"I was just *kidding*," Dawn Marie said. "What they really are is purple peewees from Pluto where your aunt and uncle live, ha ha."

She counted out five more. Then she whispered to me, "My brother's in third grade. He did mealworms last year. He says they turn into yucky brown beetles." She wiggled her fingers at my nose.

"Dawn Marie, cut it out. They do not."

"Do, too. One. Two. Three. Four. Five," she counted. "Inside these squiggles there are crunchy brown bugs. You'll see."

Every time she added five worms, I put a lid on the petri dish.

"Isn't this one cute!" She dropped it into her palm.

"No, it's not," I told her. "You can see right through it. I think it's dead."

She shook the thing onto the top of my hand. It felt like thin, thin paper.

"It's an old worm skin," she said. "The mealworm crawled out and left it behind. You can have it to keep under your pillow tonight if you give me a fig bar at snack time."

"It's bug skin?" I blew the creepy thing off my

hand. It landed on my leg, so I jumped up and down to shake it off.

When I jumped, I forgot to hold onto my purple pants.

They fell down.

They didn't fall all the way down. I grabbed too fast for that. But they fell far enough so you could see my underpants.

They were part purple.

When I put them on, my underpants were white. Now they had spots. Where my wet jeans had dripped on the purple pants, the color had soaked right through.

Not everybody saw. Mrs. Zookey was writing on the board.

Dawn Marie saw and she giggled.

Patrick saw and he laughed out loud. Then he said, so all the kids around him could hear, "I see London. I see France. I see Richard's underpants."

Kids started telling other kids. When Mrs. Zookey turned from the chalkboard, the whole room was laughing and she didn't know why.

I sat down. Why did I tell the dumb Pluto story? That just made it worse. My hands felt wet and my face felt hot.

"Settle down," Mrs. Zookey said. "Richard, Dawn Marie, it's time to deliver the worms."

Kids watched as I stood up. I kept my pants from falling by holding them tight with my right elbow. That way I could still carry a petri dish in each hand.

I took the first dishes to Table One, where my friend Ben was sitting.

"Cool pants," he said. "No kidding."

"Are these good worms?" Yolanda asked.

"Not as good as gummy ones," I told her.

I took the next ones to Table Two. One dish for me and one for Patrick. Dawn Marie had her own.

When I got to Patrick's place, he smiled at me. Then he reached out and wiggled his fingers on my ribs. It felt like a million billion rattlesnakes.

I am very, very ticklish, and Patrick knows it.

I had to push him away. I had to. And when I did, the petri dishes flew right out of my hands.

The one with my name on it popped up and then plopped down flat on Table Two.

Patrick's dish popped up, but it did not fall flat. It flipped high into the air. It turned upside down. The lid dropped off. The oats and the apple and the worms rained out. The dish crashed. The stuff inside fell *kazaam*.

And that's not all that fell. When I pushed Patrick's hands away, guess what? My elbow let go of my pants. They dropped again.

This time, just about everybody in the room saw the purple underpants. And they laughed.

Everybody laughed but Mrs. Zookey. And she looked like she wanted to.

It was a big mess. I grabbed my pants up, but the oatmeal and apple and worms were still down.

To save them I crawled under the table. If I could have, I would have stayed there forever. I wanted to close my eyes and disappear. But

Patrick crawled under with me. He pretended to look for stuff, too, but he didn't.

He grinned. "You may be part purple person from Pluto," he said, "but I know what else you are."

I found a mealworm and waved it in front of his nose.

He grinned even bigger. "You shed," he said. Then he started to sing: "Richard's pants are falling down, falling down, falling down. Richard's pants are falling down. He's part . . . mealworm."

3.

Squirms

One thing I know. A bug in a rug hides out.

The apple chunk was easy to find. I scraped up most of the oatmeal. But most of the worms had wiggled away.

When Patrick started singing the song at me again, I shoved him back on his bottom. Maybe he squooshed a mealworm. I only found four. The other one was lost in the loopy green rug forest.

Teachers don't see everything. Mrs. Zookey didn't see Patrick tickle me in the ribs. She just thought I dropped the worms. And the outer space pants.

Patrick stopped looking.

When he sat down with his petri dish, I crawled to the cabinets along the wall, calling as I went, "Here, mealworm."

The supply cabinet has lots of good stuff in it. Maybe it would have a spare belt to hold up my pants. I opened the doors.

There were rows of paste and tape, and boxes of paper clips. Paste was too icky. Tape was too sticky. Paper clips were too sharp. Then I saw the ball of bright yellow string.

String was just right. I stuck it in my pocket and raised my hand.

Mrs. Zookey said yes, I could go to the washroom if I hurried. By then, Dawn Marie had handed out the rest of the petri dishes.

"Don't linger," Mrs. Zookey told me. "We have mealworms to meet."

I ran to the washroom fast, and nobody

stopped me. When I got there I whipped out the string. Aunt Nannie had sewn four belt loops on the pants. I wound the string through the loops and pulled it really tight.

Most of the ball was left over, hanging out. I didn't have any scissors. I tried to bite through the string, but I had a loose front tooth.

Somebody was coming down the hall. Maybe they were on their way to the washroom. I didn't want anybody to see me winding yellow string around my pants.

And besides, the mealworms were waiting.

So I tied a knot fast. Then I stuck the ball of yellow string into my pocket.

My T-shirt hung down so far you couldn't see the string. In the hall, I waved my arms high. The pants didn't fall.

I ran back into the room, waving my arms to show I could. Nobody laughed. Everything was fine again.

I sat down at Table Two.

"Okay, folks," Mrs. Zookey said when she saw me, "let's have one minute of silent time.

You can use it to think about names for your mealworms."

She turned the dial on her big desk timer. *Click, click, click, click, click.*

I looked at my worms through the clear lid. In just one minute of *click, click, click* I had named them all. They were Wiggly, Waggly, Peewee (who was little), Uncle Ken (who was big), and U (who was curled up under a hill of oatmeal).

"Everyone gets a booklet," Mrs. Zookey said, passing them out. "Write your name on it. Then draw a picture of one of your mealworms on the first page. Be sure to count the legs and put them in the right places on your picture. Over the next few weeks you will write in the booklet about what happens to your mealworms."

"I know what happens," Patrick said. "Their skins fall off."

Patrick knows a lot.

"They turn into beetles," Dawn Marie said.

"Your mealworms will change," Mrs. Zookey told us. "They will go through three stages.

What you see now is the first stage. It's called a larva." She wrote the word on the board and drew a line under it.

"Over the next few weeks, as it eats a lot of oatmeal, the larva will get too big for its skin. The larva will crawl right out with brand-new skin on. Several times it will shed its old, dry skin. You'll find the skin in your dishes."

"I bet they get cold," Yolanda said.

"Can you think of any rules for taking care of your mealworms?" Mrs. Zookey asked.

"Don't let them run away."

"Don't throw them on the rug," Patrick said. "Can I have one more? I've only got four now."

"Don't hurt them," Ben called from Table One.

"Keep all that in mind," Mrs. Zookey said. "Now, ladies and gentlemen, take off the lids and meet your mealworms."

I took off my lid. Then I reached in and picked one up. Uncle Ken. I put him on my little finger, and he walked all the way around it. He tickled, but I didn't mind. Then he headed down the valley between my fingers.

Patrick hit the table with his fist. All three of our petri dishes jumped.

"It's an earthquake," he said. "It's a mealworm earthquake."

"Cut it out," I told him. "Two of my guys are asleep."

"I was trying to make one jump out of his skin," Patrick said.

"Wow!" Dawn Marie pointed. "I put Crystal in the top of the petri dish, and it's like she's on an ice rink. She'll make the mealworm Olympics."

"You think it's true there's a beetle inside them?" Patrick asked her.

"Absolutely positively," she told him. "My brother said so, and he's in third grade."

"Mine ran a race," Ben called.

"Who won?"

"King Kong. He's the only one who moved."

I put Uncle Ken on a ruler to see how long he was. Two centimeters. Then I turned the ruler upside down. He stayed on it and kept walking. "My guy's an acrobat," I told Ben.

Then I counted Uncle Ken's feet. He had six,

all in his front part. I took a brown crayon and drew a picture of him in the booklet. If he told jokes, I didn't hear them.

"Hey, look." Patrick poked me. "When I hold Snarky by his tail he goes crazy. Look at him wiggle. He likes it. He couldn't move like that with a beetle inside him."

"He'd like it best if you didn't tease him," I said.

"Almost recess time," Mrs. Zookey announced. "Count your mealworms. Make sure they're all in your petri dishes. Then put the lids back on."

"Wait, and you'll see," Dawn Marie told Patrick.

"I don't want to wait," he said. "I'm going to look."

"How are you going to look?"

"I could squeeze him open."

"You wouldn't dare."

"Wouldn't I?"

"Mrs. Zookey!" Dawn Marie called.

"Joke," Patrick told her. "Joke."

"Line up for recess," Mrs. Zookey said.

As we walked out the door I heard Patrick behind me. He said, "I've got an idea. Let's play Mealworm at recess. We'll make Richard It. He'll be Larva. We'll tickle him, and he'll shed his purple skin."

4.

Larva Legs

At recess, Ben and I played catch with a kick-ball.

My pants stayed up fine.

Then, just as the bell rang, Patrick ran by. I dodged him, so he yanked at Ben's T-shirt instead. "Larva Legs, you're It," he said. "Get Richard."

Ben bounced the ball to him.

Patrick caught it and threw it to me.

I threw it back, and he tossed it high in the air.

"I get to pick another worm," Patrick told us as we headed back inside. "Mrs. Zookey said I could. I'm going to get a big fat one. I'm going to call him Spike."

Back in our room, some kids were lined up at the sink to wash their hands. The rest were already eating.

After recess is snack time. You can take a cracker from the snack jar or bring stuff from home. The only rule is No Candy. Once I took a baggie full of Berry B'oats. But I found out they're no fun when they can't float in milk.

On Monday I'd brought a bunch of fig bars in my jacket pocket. I had two left.

Dawn Marie let me take a huge handful of her cheddar popcorn. At Table One Ben was eating green grapes. He tossed them in the air one at a time and caught them on his tongue. He only missed three.

I ate all but a corner of my first fig bar. That I

tossed under the table for the lost worm to have for supper. Then, just as I was pulling the pocket fuzz off my second bar, I heard the *whrrrrrr* of the overhead projector.

"Finish up your snacks," Mrs. Zookey said. "Your Book Buddies will be here soon. I have a special project for you."

Once a week, kids from fifth grade come to our room and we read to each other. Sometimes they write stories for us. Sometimes we write stories for them. Their stories are scarier than ours.

We learn other stuff from them, too. Dawn Marie's Book Buddy, Kayla, taught her how to make tap-dancing shoes out of sneakers. You push a big bunch of thumbtacks into the toes. That's how. Mrs. Zookey made her take them out.

My Book Buddy is a boy named Mario. All the fifth graders were there but him.

"Mario threw up in the hall," a kid told me. "He's at the nurse. Maybe he'll get here later."

Whatever we were going to do, the overhead projector was part of it. It was still whirring.

Nobody went near it. When the overhead's on, Mrs. Zookey always says, "Don't touch the overhead. It will burn you. We *really* need a new one."

"Welcome, fifth graders," Mrs. Zookey said. "I thought we'd do something different today. This should help you get to know each other even better."

Since I was Teacher's Pet, she gave me sheets of paper to pass out. Each page had two big circles on it.

"These are called Venn diagrams," Mrs. Zookey said. "You're going to fill them out with your Book Buddies. You're going to find out how you're alike. And how you're different. Have any of you done these before?" she asked.

All of the fifth graders raised their hands.

None of the second graders did. Except Patrick, and he only raised it a little way.

She put one on the overhead projector so we could all see it at the same time.

"Don't touch the overhead," she told us again. "It will burn you."

All together the second graders said, "We *really* need a new one." Everybody laughed. Even Mrs. Zookey.

"Anybody want to tell how a Venn diagram works?" she asked.

Patrick didn't raise his hand. His Book Buddy did. Her name is Galaxy. She is a lot bigger and smarter than he is. Patrick wouldn't dare tease Galaxy. He would never ever call *her* Larva Legs.

"It's like this," Galaxy said. "See those two circles. One of them will be about me, okay? The other one will tell about this short person in the bow tie."

Patrick turned red. He wears a red bow tie every day.

"See where the circles hang over each other?"

We could see it on the screen.

"That's where we're supposed to list what Practically Perfect Patrick and I have in common. Right now nothing comes to mind. There must be something."

"Let's try," Mrs. Zookey said.

"I'm a boy and she's a girl," Patrick said. "But that's how we're different."

Mrs. Zookey wrote it down.

"We're both humans. You are, aren't you, Patrick?" Galaxy asked him.

Mrs. Zookey wrote it down.

"I'm brown and he's white."

"Do you like eggplant?" Patrick asked her.

"It's my favorite. Gooey eggplant parmigiana."

"Ouch," Mrs. Zookey yelped. She stuck her finger in her mouth. "I burned myself."

Everybody went "Ohooooooo."

"Don't touch the overhead," a kid said, but it was too late for that.

"What else do you have in common?" Mrs. Zookey asked, and she blew on her burn.

"We both like science fiction."

"The weirder the better."

Mrs. Zookey wrote it down.

"I don't like silly jokes."

"I do." Patrick crossed his eyes.

"I've got three sisters."

"I've got one."

"Slow down," Mrs. Zookey said. "I can't keep up. I'll put down one sister in the middle because you both have one. Then I'll list the two extra sisters on Galaxy's side. There. You see how it works?"

Most everybody saw how it worked and started filling in the blanks. Everybody but me.

"Where's Mario?" Mrs. Zookey asked.

"Late," I told her. "I'll do one with somebody else."

Everybody else was busy, so I sat down at my desk and stared at my mealworms.

Mrs. Zookey hurried off, blowing on her finger. The overhead projector went *whrrrrrr.*

Uncle Ken was crawling upside down on the lid of the petri dish.

"Uncle Ken," I told my mealworm, "you are amazing. I'll do my Venn diagram with you."

He didn't say yes. But he didn't say no. I wrote our names in the blanks. I couldn't tell if his eyes were brown like mine, though, or ask about his sisters. I couldn't even find out if he was a he. I finished early.

Patrick and Galaxy finished early, too. She wandered off and sat in the bathtub in the reading corner. Patrick opened his petri dish. He took out a mealworm.

He held it up by its tail, and it wiggled.

"Say hello to my new mealworm, Spike," Patrick said. "Dawn Marie, watch me."

"Stop it, Patrick. You're mean," she told him.

"I'm not going to hurt him. I just want to see through him." He headed straight for the overhead projector. "Everybody, look."

Mrs. Zookey was running water on her finger, but everybody else looked at Patrick.

He dropped the mealworm onto the overhead projector. It landed next to the Venn diagram. It landed right by "yes silly jokes."

We didn't see through the worm. We did see it big and dark on the screen. It wiggled. It was funny. It wiggled a lot.

"Look at Spike go," Patrick said.

And then it stopped wiggling. It totally stopped.

Patrick looked down from the big screen worm to the little real one.

"Oh, no," he moaned. "Oh, no." And he reached over to get it. When he did that, his arm touched the side of the overhead projector, and he yelped.

"It's too hot," Dawn Marie said.

And Patrick started to cry.

"It *is* too hot," he said. "It *is*. I hurt it. I made it burn."

It wasn't his arm, either, that made him cry.

It was Spike.

Patrick picked Spike up and put him in the palm of his hand.

Patrick looked at us. And then he looked at Spike again.

Spike was all curled up.

The overhead *was* too hot.

Spike was fried.

5.

I Didn't Mean To

Spike was fried, all right.

"I'm sor-sor-sorry," Patrick sobbed.

Mrs. Zookey gave Patrick a hug. Still, Patrick would not stop crying. "I did-did-didn't mean to. I didn't want to." His nose was running. "I just wanted to see him *big*."

Mrs. Zookey turned the overhead off. The *whrrrrrr* stopped. The only noise in the room was Patrick crying.

"You all think I'm mean," he said. "You hate me."

"Look, it's just a mealworm." Galaxy had climbed out of the reading bathtub.

Maybe so, but I was glad it wasn't Uncle Ken. I checked on him. He had crawled under the oatmeal with U and Peewee.

"Mealworms are pet food," Galaxy went on. "I feed them to my lizards every day. They chew them up like little hot dogs."

"But Spike had a *name!*" Patrick said.

I had a name, but Patrick was always teasing *me.*

"Did you hurt yourself?" Mrs. Zookey asked. "Let's run some cold water on that burn."

"Cold water won't help Spike." Patrick held out the fried mealworm. He snuffled again. Then he looked at it closer. "I don't see the beetle inside," he said.

"Of course not, silly," Galaxy told him. "It takes time to turn into a beetle. It goes from larva to pupa to beetle. That takes weeks. Larva to pupa to beetle. You've just got to wait. I mean, it's like, *you're* not going to be six feet tall with a big beard tomorrow."

"Poor Spike, he'll never be a pupa."

I thought he was going to cry again.

"It's all right, Patrick," Mrs. Zookey told him. "Choose another mealworm. And this time it stays in its dish until we all take the lids off. Okay?"

"Okay," Patrick said. He snuffled again. "I'll name it Spike Two."

He and Galaxy and I headed over to the carton of mealworms.

"Next month they'll be beetles," Galaxy told him. "You'll love them."

"I wish I could be six feet tall next month with a beard like Santa Claus."

"That'd be the scariest science fiction ever," I said.

Patrick picked out a worm and put it in his dish.

"Excellent," he said.

"Maybe," Galaxy told him, "I'll write about how Spike Two turns into a small nerdy boy. I like your pants, by the way, Richard."

A bell rang. "Thanks, fifth graders," Mrs.

Zookey said. "Don't forget to bring your stories next week."

"So long, Patrick." Galaxy waved. "I might do another one about a hairy green caterpillar. It can't turn into a butterfly, so it turns into butter*milk*."

Fifth graders are seriously weird.

"Everybody, put your Venn diagrams on my desk," Mrs. Zookey said. "And, Richard, would you hand out these math sheets?" She gave me a stack of them, and I started around the room.

Patrick took his diagram and mine. He looked down at mine and then back up at me. And then he started to laugh. "Hey, everybody," he called, "look at Richard!"

He pointed at my purple pants. I looked down at them. They were still purple. But that wasn't new. I'd had them on all morning. Except when they'd been off.

I turned away and kept handing out the math sheets, one on each desk.

When I looked back, a *lot* of kids were pointing. At me.

"Guess what?" Ben called. "You've got a tail. You've got a long, yellow tail."

"It's hanging," Dawn Marie said, "out of your purple pants from Pluto."

I looked. And it was true.

The ball of string had fallen out of my pocket. The yellow string that was keeping my pants from falling down was trailing me around the room.

"I guess people from outer space grow tails," Ben said. "Instead of larva, pupa, and beetle, it goes purple pants, yellow tail, and then, who knows what next."

Everybody laughed. Me, too. I mean, it was just a joke. Ben told it.

"I've got an alligator that will bite it off," Patrick said.

"Patrick," Mrs. Zookey warned.

We all stepped back. Patrick is trouble.

He reached into his desk and pulled out an alligator. It was a scissors alligator. He opened its jaws wide over the string. When he snapped them shut, my long yellow tail fell on the floor.

Kids clapped.

Mrs. Zookey wound the string back onto the ball as we all sat down.

"You know that Venn diagram of yours?" Patrick asked me. "What I want to know is . . ."

But Mrs. Zookey made us lock our lips and throw away the key while we worked on the math sheets.

I was about to start on the third problem when the buzzer rang. It was a call from the office.

"Oh, dear, Richard, I'm sorry. It's been a busy day, I know, but it *is* Teacher's Pet's job to go to the office."

I didn't care.

"In fact," she went on, "I think this may be something special for you."

Special for me! That was good.

I hurried down the hall. My purple corduroy pants went *rufff rufff rufff* as I ran.

But then I slowed down.

What if special wasn't good?

What could special be, anyway?

I stopped for a drink at the water fountain. I touched the fuzzy rabbit pictures taped on the hall wall.

Then I slowly ruffed my way to the office.

When I opened the office door, I knew what special meant.

It meant bad.

It meant awful.

It meant terrible.

It meant that my real Uncle Ken was sitting on a chair with his ten-gallon hat on his head and a brown bag in his lap.

"Your mom called ahead," he said. "It's all right. Your teacher said I could come."

He picked up the bag.

"It's for you," he said.

6.

Uncle Ken, Meet Uncle Ken

Uncle Ken took off his big hat.

"I hope you don't mind my coming," he said. "Seemed to me you'd like to have this."

He held out the bag. I didn't take it.

"I talked to your teacher on the phone. You were out at recess, I think. She said I could stop by and meet your class. If that's okay with you."

It was not okay with me. He would try to make everybody laugh. He would go, "Huf, huf, huf." And besides, I'd told them he was from Pluto.

Uncle Ken had a name tag on his plaid shirt. When you visit our school you have to wear one. His tag said "Uncle Ken."

"We're doing math sheets," I said.

"I'm pretty good at math," he told me. And he waited.

"All right," I said, "if you want to."

"How about opening this now?" he asked as we walked down the hall.

Maybe it had socks in it with pink and orange and red stripes. Maybe he'd want me to put them on. "No thanks," I said.

This was going to be bad. Somebody would tell a Pluto joke.

"Kids in my class sometimes make up stories," I told him.

He laughed and put his cowboy hat back on. "So do I," he said. "Your Aunt Nannie says I tell too many."

I walked into the room first. Everybody looked up. They were very quiet.

"This is my Uncle Ken," I said.

He just about filled the doorway. He nodded and stepped in.

Mrs. Zookey shook his hand. "My," she said, "I wonder if you'll grow this tall, Richard. You certainly do look like your uncle."

Not! I thought.

I waited at the door. Maybe he'd seen enough. Maybe he'd just go.

"There's room at Richard's table," Mrs. Zookey told him. "Why don't you join him there? It's only a few minutes to lunch time. There's an adult-sized chair by the window."

"I'll just take this one," he said.

Uncle Ken was going to sit in Sarah's chair.

"Will you fit?"

"I reckon."

Uncle Ken sat down. Patrick stared at him hard.

"Are you *really* from outer space?" Patrick whispered.

"Patrick!" Dawn Marie said. "That's not nice."

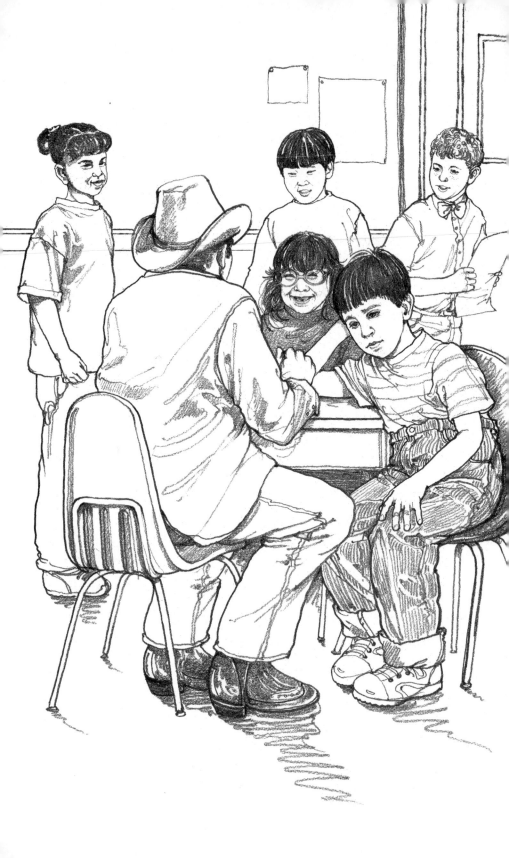

Uncle Ken didn't seem to mind. "No, young man, I'm from Texas, but I've often thought I'd like to go to the moon. I'd sure like to hop around those craters. How about you?"

"I'd rather go to Texas," Patrick told him. He did another math problem and then he looked under the table.

"Do you wear special shoes when you walk?" he asked.

"Just my cowboy boots," Uncle Ken told him. "I've got horses back home."

Patrick leaned down to look closer. "Then how do you do it?" he asked.

"Patrick, stop that!" I said. "Do *what?*"

Kids who'd turned in their math sheets were hanging around Table Two looking at Uncle Ken, waiting for the lunch bell.

"I read your Venn diagram," Patrick told me. "It said that your Uncle Ken walks on the ceiling." He sat back and crossed his arms. He looked at me and then at Uncle Ken.

Uncle Ken laughed. "Kids in your class *do* tell stories," he said.

"Richard *said*. I can show you." Patrick stood up.

"No, that was just my . . ." But I couldn't tell them. How could I say that Uncle Ken was a mealworm?

Patrick sat back down. "Under that hat," he said to Uncle Ken, "do you have feelers on your head? You know, like antennae?"

"Patrick's silly," Dawn Marie explained. "We're not all like that."

"Feelers?" Uncle Ken started to huf. He huffed so much that even more kids gathered round. "Nope," he told Patrick, "no antennae, but I've got mighty big ears." He took his hat off, showed his head to Patrick, and ran his fingers through his hair.

Patrick went to Mrs. Zookey's desk, shuffled through the papers, and came back with my Venn diagram.

"Right here." He poked the paper with his finger. "Right here it says Uncle Ken has feelers and walks on the ceiling."

"Two minutes to bell time," Mrs. Zookey called. "Everybody clear your desks and get ready for lunch. If you haven't already turned in your math sheets, bring them to me now."

"It says *what?*" Dawn Marie grabbed the paper from him.

"I was talking about a different Uncle Ken," I told them.

"It says you've got no bones." Dawn Marie waved the sheet in the air and giggled.

"A *different* Uncle Ken," I said, but they weren't listening to me.

Lots of kids were at Table Two now. And Mrs. Zookey was just smiling over at us, like everybody was being so *nice* to our visitor.

He grinned and tipped his hat to her.

"Richard," Dawn Marie said, looking at my diagram, "it says right here that your Uncle Ken has four more legs than you do. That means he'd have *six*."

We all looked at his legs.

"Huf, huf, huf," Uncle Ken laughed even bigger. "Huf, huf, huf." This time he laughed the way he does when he's going to tell a joke.

"Well, I don't know about that," he said. "I

walked here all the way from the parking lot. It's hundreds of yards, thousands of inches away, but I only moved two feet." He pointed at his boots. "*These* two feet."

"Huf, huf, huf," he went, and the kids around the table laughed with him.

Dawn Marie handed the diagram to Uncle Ken.

"You know," he said, "this Ken sure doesn't sound much like me."

"That's because it isn't you." I took the lid off the petri dish, dug around in the oatmeal, and fished out the biggest mealworm. I held him up by his tail, and he wiggled.

"Stop that," Patrick said. "You'll hurt him."

I put him on my palm and held him out. "He's got six legs and two antennae. He's got no bones. And if he told jokes, I know one he'd tell. Knock, knock."

"What do you mean?" Dawn Marie asked.

"*Knock, knock!*"

"Who's there?" Patrick said.

"Ken."

"Ken who?"

"Ken't you guess?"

I knew my uncle Ken liked to laugh. But I didn't know him very well. Maybe he liked to get mad, too. Maybe he could get really, really mad. At me.

"You mean . . ." Dawn Marie started.

I held out my hand to show it to them.

The lunch bell rang.

"Meet Uncle Ken," I said, "the mealworm." I looked down at my purple pants. And I waited to see how mad my real Uncle Ken would be.

7.

A Holdup

All the kids but Table Two ran to get in line.

"You named your mealworm Uncle Ken? After *him?*" Dawn Marie pointed at my uncle's nose. "That's gross."

"No fair," Patrick said. "First Uncle Ken lives on Pluto and now he lives in a petri dish."

"Why?" Dawn Marie asked.

"He's my biggest mealworm," I whispered, but I still couldn't look up.

Uncle Ken wasn't laughing his usual huf, huf, huf. But I couldn't see if smoke was coming out of his ears, either.

Then I felt a hand land on my head. It was big. It was Uncle Ken's. Was he going to pick me up by my hair and shake me? Where was Mrs. Zookey?

I looked at his cowboy boots.

I looked at Patrick. He wanted to save fried worms. What about saving *me!*

"Well, I'll tell you right now," I heard the real Uncle Ken say, "this is a first for me—a worm named Ken. I'm proud you thought of me, Richard. I can tell he's one fine animal. You've got to keep him fed real good, though. We Kens get hungry." He gave me a pat on the head.

My hand was shaking. My worm must have thought he was on a trampoline. I picked him out of the palm of my hand and stuck him back in his clear plastic house. I shut the lid.

"Time for lunch. Oats again," I told him.

"Says here on this fancy diagram," Uncle Ken

said, pointing to my Venn, "that this mealworm that's named after me sheds his skin. Is that right?"

I nodded.

"It also says you shed your pants." He looked at me. "Does that mean the new purple pants your Aunt Nannie made?"

I nodded.

"Stand up. Let's see."

The yellow string around my waist had been stretching all morning. I could feel it getting loose. I was afraid to stand up. I shook my head.

Mrs. Zookey had been listening. She came over to the table. "You were right. The pants are a problem for Richard," she said to him. "I was glad you called."

Uncle Ken had talked to Mrs. Zookey on the telephone. They had talked about how my pants were falling down. I wanted to crawl under the table again.

"Here you go, Richard," he said. He picked up the brown bag from my desk and handed it to me.

I took the bag and pushed it into my desk.

"Open it," Dawn Marie told me. "It's a gift."

"Later," I said. No telling what it was.

"Now," Patrick said, "or I'll open it for you."

"Go ahead," Mrs. Zookey told me. "It's all right."

I waited for Uncle Ken to tell his joke. He was smiling, and it was a joke kind of smile.

I pulled the bag out, opened it, and looked inside. Whatever it was, it was red. Bright red.

I took the present out and waved it in the air. It didn't look like a joke. I knew what it was. I'd never had one before, but I knew what it was. It was a pair of suspenders. And they were the reddest red I'd ever seen.

If my mother was there, she would have said, "What do you say, Richard?" So I said it. "Thank you, Uncle Ken. Thank you very much. They are really red."

"You like them?" Uncle Ken grinned. "You know what they're as red as?" he asked.

Here it came. The joke. The Uncle Ken joke.

He was like a sled heading down a hill. You

couldn't stop him, so you might as well jump on.

"Red as a fire engine?" I tried.

He shook his head.

"Red as blood," Patrick said. "Thick, ooshy, sticky . . ."

"Red as Mrs. Zookey's lipstick," Dawn Marie tried.

"Nope. They are red as the stuff you put on hot dogs," Uncle Ken told us.

"Ketchup?" I asked.

"That's what they're for," he said, "to catch-up your pants so they won't fall down."

And all of us went, "Huf, huf, huf, huf." Mrs. Zookey, too.

"They're just right," she told me. "Tuck in your shirt, Richard. I'll clip them to your pants in the back. You clip them in front. Patrick, get out your alligator. It can bite off the yellow string belt."

Patrick's alligator opened its jaws and snapped the string. The string fell down. The pants stayed up.

"Your mom and I were all for bringing you your jeans, but they'd got caught in a flood," Uncle Ken said. "Besides, your Aunt Nannie wouldn't hear of it. 'The boy would cry,' she told us. 'He just loves those purple pants.'"

"Everybody noticed them," Dawn Marie said.

"They had their ups and downs," I told him.

"I bet they did." He laughed. "Your mom gave us your belt to bring to you. When she got to work, she called the school to say we'd stop by. But your Aunt Nannie wouldn't hear of it. Said the belt wasn't special enough."

I looped my thumbs under the suspenders, pulled them out, and let them go snap. Then I did it again. "I like these," I told him.

"Well, Nannie and I, we went to the mall as soon as it opened," he said. "It was either these or an orange pair. But I couldn't think of a good orange knock-knock."

"They're just fine." Mrs. Zookey looked me over. "I think Richard is all set."

"That's what I am, too," Uncle Ken said. "Set to go. Time to pick up Nannie. She's shopping

for yarn. Going to knit a big purple sweater to give your dad." He stood up.

"For my dad? Purple, like my pants?"

He nodded. "Real bright. Like father, like son." He started for the door. "Glad to meet you all—especially my namesake."

Then he turned back. "Tell you what, Richard," he said, "after school, let's you and me go fishing on that Green Lake. I'll check it out. If we catch a good-sized one, I'll fry it up for dinner."

Uncle Ken tipped his cowboy hat to us and to Mrs. Zookey, and then he left.

On the way to lunch I hopped down the hall like a kangaroo. My new red suspenders worked. "They're so red, they ketchup my pants," I told Patrick and Dawn Marie.

They laughed at the old joke.

Kids in the hall laughed at me. I still looked funny.

"My Uncle Ken is going away day after tomorrow," I said.

"Which Uncle Ken?" Patrick asked.

"The one with bones. In two weeks they'll be in Seattle. I bet Aunt Nannie will be done with my dad's sweater by then. I'll write and tell him about my purple pants."

"You'll have to wear them tomorrow, too, if your aunt and uncle are still here," Dawn Marie told me. "They went to a lot of trouble."

"But, after that, you won't have to put them on ever again," Patrick said.

"I like them." Dawn Marie looked me over. "Maybe your mother could make them smaller."

"But then I wouldn't get to wear the suspenders." I pulled them out far and snapped them. "Maybe I'll just grow fast."

Two kids passing us looked at me and giggled.

"You do look silly," Patrick said.

"I know," I said. "Knock, knock."

"Who's there?"

"Ida."

"Ida who?"

"Ida wanna look silly."

"It's just that it's no fun if you do it by yourself." Dawn Marie stopped and shook her head. "Maybe if some other kids . . ."

"Don't look at me," Patrick said. "I don't have anything silly." He hurried away down the hall and then turned back. "Well, maybe one thing. For my birthday, my grandmother sent me a shirt. It's baby blue and it's too short. And it's got yellow smiley faces all over. I hid it in a closet so I wouldn't ever ever have to wear it. It's the silliest thing in the world."

"Maybe it is. Maybe it isn't," Dawn Marie said. "My mother's very *very* best friend gave me this icky green dress. It's got a gazillion green ruffles on it. My mother's very *very* best friend said it makes me look good enough to eat. I think it makes me look like a cabbage."

We were the last ones to get to the cafeteria. All the tacos were gone, so we had to take cheese sandwiches.

We also got mixed salad with ranch dressing and a red and green gummy worm on top.

Dawn Marie took the gummy worm off the

salad and put it on the edge of her tray. Patrick and I ate ours right away. We all sat down at one of the second grade tables.

"I happen to know," Dawn Marie said. "I happen to know for sure that Sarah's mother had a Raggedy Ann dress when she was little. I also happen to know that sometimes Sarah puts it on. If I tell her to, she'll wear it tomorrow. It looks even sillier when she paints a red triangle on her nose."

We all sat there eating our cheese sandwiches.

"The smiley face shirt would be awful with my red bow tie," Patrick said. "Okay, Dawn Marie, I will if you will."

Dawn Marie pushed her nose up and made a pig face. "Tomorrow is Silly Clothes Day at Table Two," she said. "I'll do it. Cross my heart and hope to die. Stick my face in lemon pie." We all three said it.

"I bet," Patrick told us, "that when we do it, they'll want a Silly Clothes Day at Table One."

"*And* Three, Four, Five, and Six." I was sure of

it. "But maybe my pants aren't funny enough. Maybe I should add this pink bunny cap."

"Knock, knock," Dawn Marie said.

"Who's there?"

"Orange."

"Orange who?"

"Orange you glad your aunt and uncle came from purple planet Pluto?"

"Positively," I said. "Knock, knock again," I said.

"Who's there?"

"Ken."

"Ken who?"

"Ken't wait," I said. "I Ken't wait until tomorrow."